In memory of my mother, who would have been so proud.

For Booth.

Special thanks to Victoria Rock, Kendra Marcus, and to Beth for being on a ferry on Lake Como.

ISBN 0-590-85919-6

Copyright © 1994 by Nina Laden.
All rights reserved. Published by Scholastic Inc., 555 Broadway, New York, NY 10012, by arrangement with Chronicle Books.

12 11 10 9 8 7 6 5 4 3 2 1   6 7 8 9/9 0 1/0

Printed in the U.S.A.   08

First Scholastic printing, January 1996

THE NIGHT I FOLLOWED THE DOG

WORDS AND PICTURES BY NINA LADEN

SCHOLASTIC INC.
NEW YORK TORONTO LONDON AUCKLAND SYDNEY

I have a dog. Nothing exotic or special, just an ordinary dog. In fact, I always thought he was a boring dog. What I mean is, he can Fetch, ROLL OVER, and shake hands, but mostly he sleeps and EATS.

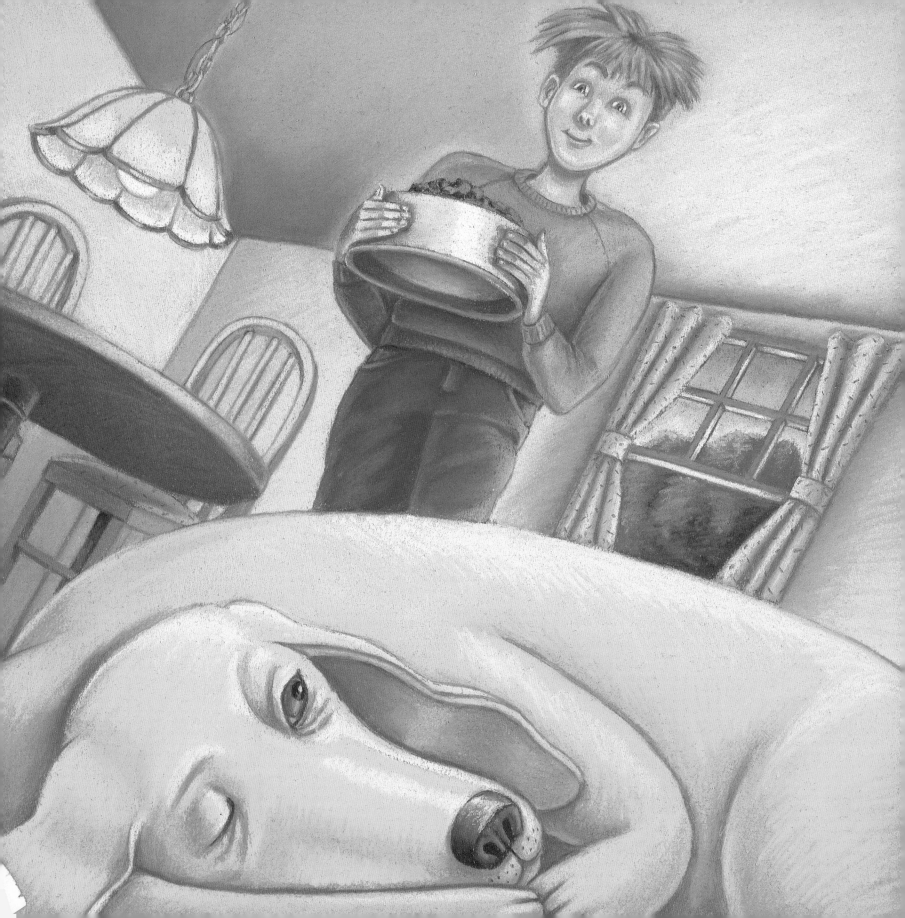

I used to think that our next-door neighbors had the best dog in the world. Their dog can sing and change the channels on the TV. Their dog always wins MEDALS in obedience school. But I don't think their dog is so great now — not since the night I followed MY dog.

Every night, I let my dog out, and he runs off into the darkness with his tail **wagging**. The next morning I let him in, and he heads straight for the food bowl. But one morning I knew something was FUNNY when I opened the door a little bit earlier than usual, and I saw my dog jump out of a LIMOUSINE . . . wearing a tuxedo.

Before I could look twice, he **DISAPPEARED** into the backyard. I opened the kitchen door and *whistled.* When he came into the house he was the same as he always is, **hungry**. I really wasn't sure that I believed what I had seen, so that night I decided to follow him.

I wore **DARK CLOTHING**, so I wouldn't be noticed, and I left my bicycle near the door, so I'd have it close by. When I let the dog out, I slipped out, too. I took out the garbage, so he wouldn't suspect anything. The dog went straight to his doghouse. I saw a light go on inside. **SLOWLY**, I snuck around the backyard, and peeked into the doghouse.

This was not the doghouse that I had helped build. Inside, there was a living room, a bathroom, and a **HUGE** closet full of Fancy clothes. The dog was in the bathroom. He was wearing a tuxedo and **Fumbling** with the bow tie. When he came out, he casually walked out of the doghouse, across the yard, and down the street.

I grabbed my bicycle and followed him. Two blocks later, I saw a **LIMOUSINE** pull over. The dog got in, and the car took off. I started pedaling **FASTER**. The car headed across town. I thought I would lose them, but luckily they were stopped by a few red lights.

There was nothing on the outside of the building, just two BRASS fire hydrants on either side of the entrance. I opened the door. At the end of the hall there was a NEON sign that said "The Doghouse." I crept closer. It looked like some kind of club. I decided to get a CLOSER look.

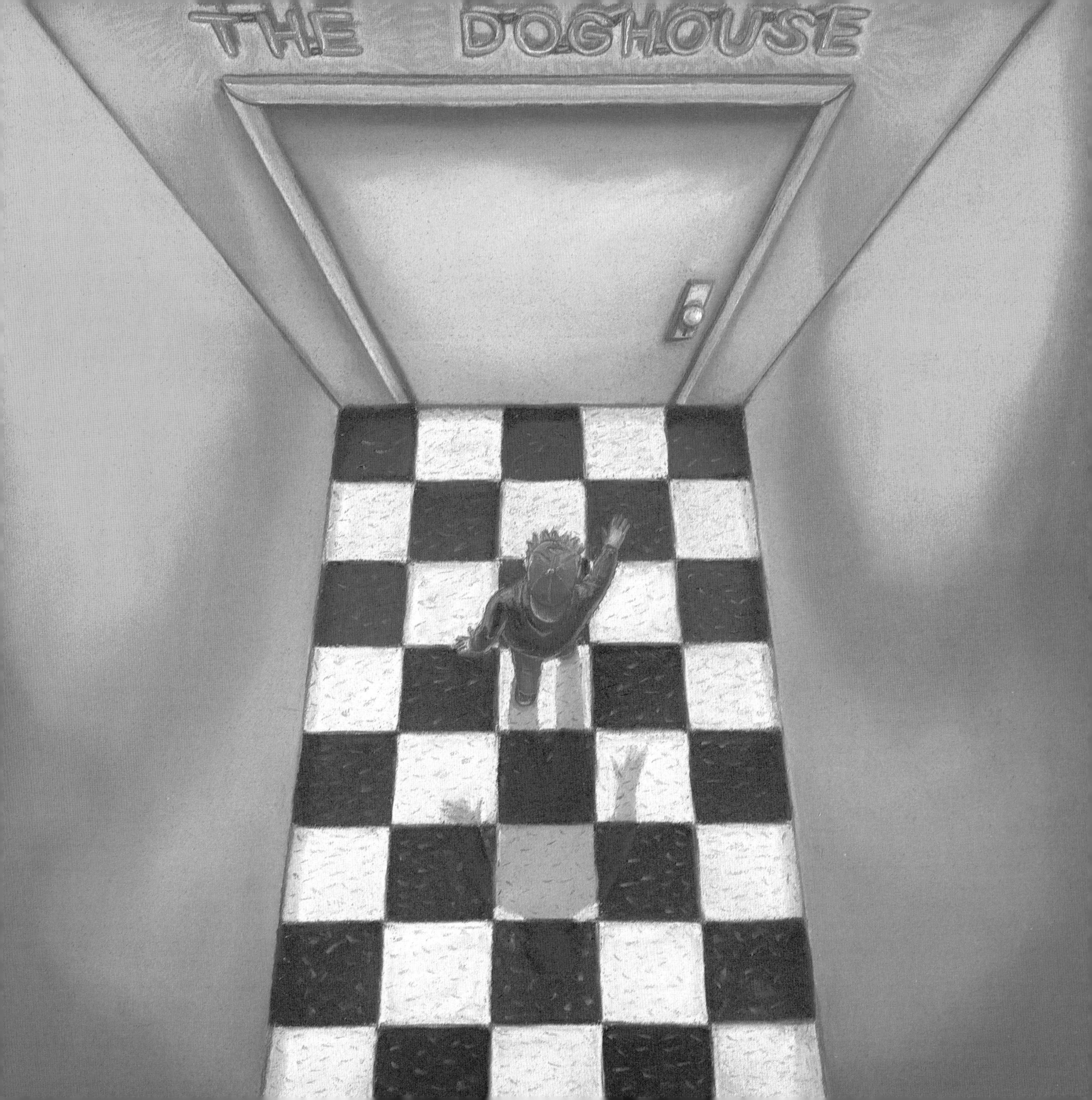
THE DOGHOUSE

The moment I opened the door two **MEAN** looking bulldogs appeared and said, "You can't come in here!" I didn't know what to say, so I said, "B-but, b-but I saw my dog ... I mean, I think my dog's in here." Just then, my dog walked over and said, "It's okay, boys, he's with me." The bulldogs said, "Sure, **Boss**. Whatever you say, **Boss**."

For a minute that seemed like forever, I waited. Then my dog said, "I knew you would find out eventually. Well, now you know. This is my place." I looked around. Finally, I asked, "What is this place?" My dog said, "This? This is a place where dogs come after a hard day. It's a place where we can **relax**. It's a place where we can talk about our problems with the MAILMAN, or with the **poodle** next door."

"See all the sofas? We can sit on the sofas here. We can get treats without having to SHAKE HANDS, ROLL OVER, or play dead. And if we want to chew on a shoe or CHASE OUR TAIL, no one will stop us. We have no masters here, no leashes, and no rolled up newspapers. This? This is a place where dogs can be dogs."

We sat down. A cocker spaniel came by and asked me if I would like a bowl of water, or some BISCUITS. Little by little, dogs of all kiNDS started coming in. Some danced, some TALKED. They all looked at me a little funny, but when they saw who I was with, they smiled, and shook my hand.

At one point, my dog waved to an afghan with a camera. She came over to our table and took a Picture of us together. Being with my dog made me feel like a movie star.

Just when I was really starting to enjoy myself, I looked at my watch. I told my dog I had to leave, or I'd get in **TROUBLE**. He nodded. I think he was about to say something, but a **Glamorous** greyhound grabbed his paw and whisked him onto the dance floor. As he was getting up, he tossed me the **PHOTO** of the two of us. Then he bowed slightly and disappeared into the **CROWD**.

It was way past my bedtime. As I pedaled home into the COOL night, I thought to myself, "Now I'm really going to be in the doghouse." But then again, that might not be so bad.

THE END